Afraid of the
DARK!

igloo

Little Polar Bear's home is big and cold and snowy.
The icebergs glimmer... the water sparkles...

...and Little Polar Bear plays with her friends all day long.

She loves rolling in the crisp, white snow until her fur sparkles.
She loves diving into the blue, swirly water and chasing fish.

There's just one thing that Little Polar Bear doesn't like . . .

the night is very,

very,

very,

DARK!

All the polar bears are gathering to welcome the new moon.
Tonight is a very special night.

"Come with me, little Polar Bear,"
says Daddy.
"It will be great fun."

"We will sing songs.

We will dance until the sun
rises over the icebergs.

We will dive in the water
and chase the sleepy seals.

And the Wise Old Bear will tell us about his adventures."

But Little Polar Bear is too frightened to join in the fun.

So Daddy goes to welcome the new moon by himself.

The night is full of SCary noises!

The wind MOANS...

...and HOWLS

...and WAILS!

Little Polar Bear wants to run after Daddy.
But the night is full of **fearsome monsters!**

Strange shadows creep around the cave!

Little Polar Bear is afraid.
The night is **too dark!**

"I'll **never** be able to welcome the new moon," says Little Polar Bear. "I'm just not **brave** enough."

Big tears roll down her nose and plop onto the ice.

Then she hears a heavy paw-step scrunching in the snow.
Little Polar Bear is **so scared!**

It's the Wise Old Bear!
"Don't cry, Little Polar Bear," he smiles.
"There's nothing to be scared of.
Come outside, and you can see something wonderful."

Little Polar Bear shivers and shakes.
But she goes outside with the Wise Old Bear.

Polar Bear is frightened.

she looks up . . .

slowly,

slowly,

But slowly,

"Oh! The night is beautiful!"
whispers Little Polar Bear.

"The moon and the stars
are your friends," says the Wise Old Bear.
"You can tell them all your secrets."

"They have watched over bears for hundreds and hundreds of years,
and they will watch over you, too."

Polar Bear runs to meet Daddy.

"You're here!" he smiles.

They jump and dive and play.

In the water.

They sing and dance in the moonlight.

Daddy gives Little Polar Bear a **big** bear hug.
"You did something very special," he says.

"You did something even though you were **scared**.
Do you know what that makes you, Little Polar Bear?"